BEST LOVED
FAIRY TALES
OF
WALTER CRANE

THE GROLIER SOCIETY INC. • NEW YORK

CONTENTS

THE HIND IN THE WOOD

6

THE HIND IN THE WOOD

Once upon a time there was a King and Queen who were very happy together, but great sorrow was felt that they had no child. One day when the Queen was sitting by a fountain, a large crab appeared, and said, "Great Queen, you shall have your wish." The crab then changed into a handsome little old woman. She led the Queen through a path in the wood which she had never seen before, although she had been in the wood a thousand times.

The Queen's astonishment was increased by the sight of a palace of diamonds. The gates opened, and six fairies appeared. They all made a courtesy to the Queen, and each presented her with a flower of precious stones. There was a rose, a tulip, an anemone, a columbine, a carnation, and a pomegranate. "Madam," said they, "we are delighted to announce that you will have a beautiful Princess, whom you will call Desiree. Send for us the moment she is born, for we wish to endow her with all good qualities; hold the bouquet, and name each flower, thinking of us, and we will be instantly in your chamber."

8

The Queen returned to the court, and soon after, a Princess was born, whom she named Desiree; she took the bouquet, named the flowers one after another, and all the fairies arrived. They took the little Princess upon their knees and kissed her, one endowing her with virtue, another with wit, a third with beauty, the next with good fortune, the fifth with good health, and the last with the gift of doing everything well which she undertook.

The Queen thanked them for the wonderful things they had given the little Princess. All of a sudden a crab entered that was so large that the door was scarcely wide enough for her to pass through. "Ah! ungrateful Queen," said the crab, "have you so soon forgotten the Fairy of the Fountain, and the service I gave you by introducing you to my sisters! You have invited them all, and I alone am neglected!" The Queen asked her pardon; and the fairies, who feared she would endow the child with misery and misfortune, tried to help the Queen appease her. "Very well," she said; "I will not do all the mischief to Desiree I had intended. However, I warn you that if she sees the light of day before she is fifteen, it will perhaps cost her her life."

As soon as the crab had left, the Queen asked the fairies to save her daughter from the threatened evil, and they decided to build a palace without doors or windows, and to educate the Princess there till the fatal period passed. Three taps of a wand produced this grand palace, in which there was no light but that of wax candles and lamps; but there were so many of these that it was as light as day. The Princess's intelligence and skill enabled her to learn very quickly, while her wit and beauty charmed everybody. The Queen would never have lost sight of her, if her duty had not obliged her to be near the King.

The good fairies every now and then went to see the Princess. As the time drew near for her to leave the palace, the Queen had her portrait painted, and sent it to the greatest courts of the world. There was not a prince who did not admire it but there was one who could never leave it. He shut himself up, and talked to it as though it could understand him.

The name of this Prince was Andrew. Andrew's father, the King, who now hardly ever saw his son, inquired as to what prevented his appearing as cheerful as usual. Some of the courtiers told him they feared the Prince would go out of his mind; for he remained for days shut up in his room, talking as though he had some lady with him. The King sent for his son, and asked him why he was behaving so strangely. The Prince threw himself at his father's feet, and said, "I confess that I am desperately in love with Princess Desiree, and wish to marry her." He ran for the portrait, and brought it to the King, who said, "Ah! my dear Andrew, I consent to your wish. I shall become young again when I have so lovely a Princess at my court."

The Prince begged the King to send an ambassador to Princess Desiree; and Fernando, a very elegant young nobleman, was selected.

The ambassador took his leave of the Prince, who said, "Remember, my dear Fernando, that my life depends upon this marriage. Do everything you must to bring the lovely Princess back with you."

The ambassador took with him many presents for the Princess, and also a portrait of the Prince.

On his arrival, the King and Queen were very excited; they heard of Prince Andrew's personal merits, and were happy to have found a husband for their daughter so worthy of her.

The King and Queen resolved that the ambassador should see Desiree, but the Fairy Tulip said to the Queen, "Take care, Madam, that you do not introduce Fernando to the Princess; he must not see her yet, and do not consent to let her go until she is fifteen years old. Remember, if she leaves the palace before then, some misfortune will happen to her." And the Queen promised to follow her advice.

On the ambassador's arrival, he asked to see the Princess, and was surprised that he was not allowed to do so. The King then told Fernando of the Princess's extraordinary adventure, and that there were still over three months to go until the Princess would be fifteen years old.

The ambassador, finding his attempts to obtain the Princess were useless, took leave of the King, and returned. When the Prince found he could not hope to see his dear Desiree for more than three months, he became dangerously ill. The

King was very unhappy and decided to go to the father and mother of Desiree to beg them to allow the marriage to take place immediately.

During all this time, Desiree, who had been given Prince Andrew's portrait, would spend all the day looking at it with the greatest pleasure, just as Prince Andrew would look upon her portrait. All of Desiree's attendants knew about this, particularly her maids of honor, Roselou and Jacqueline. Now, Roselou loved her dearly and was faithful; but Jacqueline had always been jealous of Desiree. Her mother had been the Princess's governess, and was now her principal lady-in-waiting, but as she doted on her own daughter, she could not wish well to Desiree.

Fernando again posted with the greatest speed to the city where Desiree's father lived, and assured the King and Queen that Prince Andrew would die if they refused him their daughter any longer. At last, they promised him that before evening they would tell him what could be done. The Queen went to her daughter's palace, and told her all that had passed. Desiree was very unhappy, but the Queen said, "Do not distress yourself, my dear; you are able to cure him. I am only worried about the threats of the Fairy of the Fountain." "Couldn't I go in a coach," she replied, "so closely shut that I could not see daylight? They might open it at night, to give me something to eat, and I should be able to arrive safely at the palace of Prince Andrew."

The King and Queen thought this was a very good idea;

and they sent for Fernando, telling him the Princess should set out instantly. The ambassador thanked their Majesties, and again returned to the Prince.

A coach was built, lined with pink and silver brocade. There were no glass windows in it; and one of the first noblemen in the kingdom had charge of the keys. And so, Desiree was locked up in the coach with her principal lady-in-waiting, Roselou and Jacqueline. Jacqueline did not like the Princess and was in love with Prince Andrew, whose picture she had seen. She told her mother she would die if the Princess's marriage took place; and the lady-in-waiting said she would try to prevent it.

The King and Queen felt no uneasiness for their daughter; but Jacqueline, who learned each night from the Princess's officers the progress they were making, urged her mother to go ahead with her plans. So about midday, when the sun was shining very brightly, she suddenly cut off the roof of the coach with a large knife. Then, for the first time, Princess Desiree saw the light of day.

She had scarcely looked at it when she suddenly turned into the form of a white hind and sprang from the coach running off to the forest where she hid herself in the shade of trees.

The Fairy of the Fountain, who had brought about this event, seemed to want to destroy the whole world. Thunder and lightning terrified the boldest, and no one remained but the lady-in-waiting, Jacqueline and Roselou. Roselou ran

into the forest after the Princess.

Jacqueline dressed herself in Desiree's richest apparel, and followed by her mother, set forth towards the city, and were met by the King and his son. The King, advancing with his court, joined the false Princess; but the moment he saw her, he gave a cry, and fell back. "What do I see?" said he. "Sire," said the lady-in-waiting, boldly advancing, "this is the Princess Desiree, with letters from the King and Queen. I also deliver into your hands the chest of jewels they gave me on setting out."

The King listened to this in silence, and the Prince, leaning upon Fernando, approached Jacqueline, who was as ugly as Desiree was beautiful. Struck with astonishment, he cried, "I am betrayed," addressing himself to the King. "What do you mean, my lord?" said Jacqueline; "you will never be deceived in marrying me." The King and Prince did not answer her; they got back on their horses and had their body-guards take the false Princess and the lady-in-waiting back to the city where they were shut up in the castle.

Prince Andrew was so overwhelmed by the shock that he could no longer remain at the court, and determined to leave it secretly to find some solitary place where he would spend the rest of his sad life. He told his plan to Fernando who he knew would follow him anywhere. He wrote a long letter to the King assuring him that the moment his mind was more at ease, he would return.

While everybody tried to console the King, the Prince and Fernando sped away. At the end of three days they found themselves in a vast forest, where the Prince, who was still ill, dismounted while Fernando went out to find some fruits for their refreshment.

It is a long time since we left the Hind in the Wood. The Fairy Tulip felt for her misfortune, and conducted Roselou towards the forest so that she might console the Princess. Roselou was looking for her dear mistress, when the hind saw her, and leaping a brook, ran up eagerly and caressed her a thousand times. Roselou looked at it carefully, and could not doubt that it was her dear Princess. Their tears affected the Fairy Tulip, who suddenly appeared. Roselou begged her to restore Desiree to her natural form. "I cannot do that," said Tulip, "but I can shorten her term of punishment. As soon as night falls she will become her lovely self; but, as soon as it is dawn, she must return to being a hind, and roam the plains and forests like the other animals."

"Follow this path," she continued, "and you will come to a little hut." So saying, she disappeared. Roselou followed her directions, and found an old woman seated by the door of the hut, finishing a straw basket. She led them into a very pretty room, in which were two little beds. As soon as it was quite dark, Desiree was no longer a hind. She embraced Roselou, and promised that she would reward her as soon as her penance had ended. The old woman knocked at the door and gave them some fruit. They then went to bed.

As soon as daylight appeared, Desiree, having become a hind again, plunged into the wood. Meanwhile, Fernando arrived at the cottage and asked the old woman for several things for his master. She filled a basket for him, and offered them shelter for the night, which was accepted.

The Prince slept restlessly, and as soon as it was day he arose and went into the forest. As he was walking he saw a hind running in the woods, and he shot an arrow at it. This hind was none other than Desiree, but her friend Tulip preserved her from being struck. The Prince lost sight of her, and being very tired, gave up the pursuit.

The next day the Prince went to the forest again, determined to find that hind and not let it get away. He walked for a long, long time until he was too tired to go any further. He lay down and went to sleep. While he was sleeping, the hind came to the spot where he lay. She crouched down a little distance from him and touched him. This awoke the Prince, who was greatly surprised to see the hind. She ran off into the woods and he followed her.

Soon she could run no longer. The Prince, seeing she had lost all her strength, cut some branches from the trees and placed her gently upon the boughs. She became very uneasy, however, as night approached. She was thinking how to escape, when the Prince left her to search for some water.

While he was gone, she stole away, and safely reached the cottage. The Prince returned as soon as he had found a spring, and looked for the hind everywhere, but in vain.

So he returned to the cottage and told Fernando about his adventure with the hind.

The next day, once again Desiree, in the form of the white hind, hid herself far away in the forest. All of a sudden she saw the Prince. She instantly fled, but as she was crossing a path, he lodged an arrow in her leg. Her strength failed and she fell. The Prince was greatly grieved to see the hind bleeding. He gathered some herbs, bound them round her leg, and made a bed of branches. He placed the hind's head upon his knees and lavished caresses upon her.

At last the time came to return to the old woman's cottage. He wanted to carry the hind back with him but felt he could not do it alone. He tied the hind to a tree and went to look for Fernando. The hind tried in vain to escape. Just then Roselou passed by the spot where she was struggling and set her free. The Prince and Fernando arrived and claimed the hind as theirs. "My lord," replied Roselou, "this hind belonged to me before she did to you. I would much sooner lose my life than her." The Prince generously gave her up.

They returned to the cottage, and the Prince went in shortly after to ask the old woman who the young lady was. The old woman replied that she did not know. But Fernando said he knew she had lived with Princess Desiree, and to be sure, he made a hole in the wall large enough to see into the next room.

Roselou was bandaging the Princess' arm, which was bleeding. They both appeared very distressed. "Alas!" said the

Princess, "must I become a hind every day, and see the Prince, the man I love, without being able to speak to him!" Fernando was astonished. He ran for the Prince, who looked through the hole, and immediately recognized the Princess. Without delay he knocked gently on the door and ran to Desiree.

"What!" he exclaimed, "was it you I injured with my arrow, in the form of a white hind?" Desiree assured him that she was all right. She spoke to him so kindly that he could not doubt her love for him. They decided they would return to the castle immediately to be married.

All this was brought about by the Fairy Tulip. The pretty house in the wood was here, and she herself was the old woman.

The Prince and the Princess were received in the castle with shouts of joy; everything was prepared for the wedding. The six fairies came to attend the ceremony; and Fernando was married to Roselou at the same time.

BEAUTY AND THE BEAST

BEAUTY AND THE BEAST

O NCE upon a time a rich Merchant, meeting with heavy
losses, had to retire to a small cottage, with his three
daughters. The two elder grumbled at this; but the youngest, named Beauty, tried to comfort her father and make
his home happy. Once, when he was going on a journey,
to try to mend his fortunes, the girls came to wish him
good-bye; the two elder told him to bring them some nice
presents on his return, but Beauty merely begged of him
to bring her a rose. When the Merchant was on his way
back he saw some fine roses, and thinking of Beauty,
plucked the prettiest he could find. He had no sooner taken
it than he saw a hideous Beast, armed with a deadly
weapon. This fierce-looking creature asked him how he

dared to touch his flowers, and talked of putting him to death. The Merchant pleaded that he only took the rose to please his daughter Beauty, who had begged of him to get her one.

On this, the Beast said gruffly, "Well, I will not take your life, if you will bring one of your daughters here to die in your stead. She must come willingly, or I will not have her. You may stay and rest in my palace until to-morrow." Although the Merchant found an excellent supper laid for him, he could not eat; nor could he sleep, although everything was made ready for his comfort. The next morning he set out on a handsome horse, provided by the Beast.

When he came near his house his children came out to greet him. But seeing the sadness of his face, and his eyes filled with tears, they asked the cause of his trouble. Giving Beauty the rose, he told her all. The two elder sisters laid all the blame on Beauty; but his sons, who had come from the forest to meet him, declared that they would go to the Beast instead. But Beauty said that as she was the cause of this misfortune, she alone must suffer for it, and was quite willing to go; and, in spite of the entreaties of her brothers, who loved her dearly, she set out with her father, to the secret joy of her two envious sisters.

When they arrived at the palace the doors opened of themselves; sweet music was heard, and they walked into a room where supper was prepared. Just as they had eaten

their supper, the Beast entered, and said in a mild tone, "Beauty, did you come here willingly to die in place of your father?" "Willingly," she answered, with a trembling voice. "So much the better for you," said the Beast; "your father can stay here to-night, but must go home on the following morning." Beauty tried to cheer her father, at parting, by saying that she would try to soften the heart of the Beast, and get him to let her return home soon. After he was gone, she went into a fine room, on the door of which was written, in letters of gold, "Beauty's Room;" and lying on the table was a portrait of herself, under which were these words: "Beauty is Queen here; all things will obey her." All her meals were served to the sound of music, and at supper-time the Beast, drawing the curtains aside, would walk in, and talk so pleasantly that she soon lost much of her fear of him. At last, he turned towards her, and said, "Am I so very ugly?" "Yes, indeed you are," replied Beauty, "but then you are so kind that I don't mind your looks." "Will you marry me, then?" asked he. Beauty, looking away, said, "Pray don't ask me." He then bade her "Good-night" with a sad voice, and she retired to her bed-chamber.

The palace was full of galleries and apartments, containing the most beautiful works of art. In one room was a cage filled with rare birds. Not far from this room she saw a numerous troop of monkeys of all sizes. They advanced to meet her, making her low bows. Beauty was

30

much pleased with them, and said she would like some of them to follow her and keep her company. Instantly two tall young apes, in court dresses, advanced, and placed themselves with great gravity beside her, and two sprightly little monkeys took up her train as pages. From this time the monkeys always waited upon her with all the attention and respect that officers of a royal household are accustomed to pay to queens.

Beauty was now, in fact, quite the Queen of the palace, and all her wishes were gratified; but, excepting at supper-time, she was always alone; the Beast then appeared, and behaved so agreeably that she liked him more and more. But to his question, "Beauty, will you marry me?" he never could get any other answer than a shake of the head from her, on which he always took his leave very sadly.

Although Beauty had everything she could wish for she was not happy, as she could not forget her father, and brothers, and sisters. At last, one evening, she begged so hard of the Beast to let her go home that he agreed to her wish, on her promising not to stay away longer than two months, and gave her a ring, telling her to place it on her dressing-table whenever she desired to go or to return; and then showed her where to find suitable clothes, as well as presents to take home. The poor Beast was more sad than ever. She tried to cheer him, saying "Beauty will soon return," but nothing seemed to comfort him. Beauty then went to her room, and before retiring to rest she took care

to place the ring on the dressing-table. When she awoke next morning, what was her joy at finding herself in her father's house, with the gifts and clothes from the palace at her bed-side.

At first she wondered where she was; but she soon heard the voice of her father, and, rushing out, she flung her arms round his neck. The father and daughter had much to say to each other. Beauty related all that had happened to her at the palace. Her father, enriched by the liberality of the Beast, had left his old house, and now lived in a very large city, and her sisters were engaged to be married to young men of good family.

When she had passed some weeks with her family, Beauty found that her sisters, who were secretly vexed at her good fortune, still looked upon her as a rival, and treated her with coldness. Besides this, she remembered her promise to the Beast, and resolved to return to him. But her father and brothers begged her to stay a day or two longer, and she could not resist their entreaties. But one night she dreamed that the poor Beast was lying dead in the palace garden; she awoke in a fright, looked for her ring, and placed it on the table. In the morning she was at the Palace again, but the Beast was nowhere to be found: at last she ran to the place in the garden that she had dreamed about, and there, sure enough, the poor Beast was, lying senseless on his back.

At this sight Beauty wept and reproached herself for

having caused his death. She ran to a fountain and sprinkled his face with water. The Beast opened his eyes, and as soon as he could speak, he said, sorrowfully, "Now that I see you once more, I die contented!". "No, no!" she cried, "you shall not die! Oh, live to be my husband, and Beauty will be your faithful wife!" The moment she had uttered these words, a dazzling light shone everywhere; the Palace windows glittered with lamps, and music was heard around. To her great wonder, a handsome young Prince stood before her, who said that her words had broken the spell of a magician, by which he had been doomed to wear the form of a Beast, until a beautiful girl should love him in spite of his ugliness. The grateful Prince now claimed Beauty as his wife. The Merchant was soon informed of his daughter's good fortune, and the Prince was married to Beauty on the following day.

THE FROG PRINCE

38

THE FROG PRINCE

IN the olden time, when wishing was having, there lived a King, whose daughters were all beautiful; but the youngest was so exceedingly beautiful that the Sun himself, although he saw her very often, was enchanted every time she came out into the sunshine.

Near the castle of this King was a large and gloomy forest, and in the midst stood an old lime-tree, beneath whose branches splashed a little fountain; so, whenever it was very hot, the King's youngest daughter ran off into this wood, and sat down by the side of this fountain; and,

when she felt dull, would often divert herself by throwing a golden ball up in the air and catching it. And this was her favourite amusement.

Now, one day it happened, that this golden ball, when the King's daughter threw it into the air, did not fall down into her hand, but on the grass; and then it rolled past her into the fountain. The King's daughter followed the ball with her eyes, but it disappeared beneath the water, which was so deep that no one could see to the bottom.' Then she began to lament, and to cry louder and louder; and, as she cried, a voice called out, "Why weepest thou, O King's daughter? thy tears would melt even a stone to pity." And she looked around to the spot whence the voice came, and saw a Frog stretching his thick ugly head out of the water. "Ah! you old water-paddler," said she, "was it you that spoke? I am weeping for my golden ball, which has slipped away from me into the water."

"Be quiet, and do not cry," answered the Frog; "I can give thee good advice. But what wilt thou give me if I fetch thy plaything up again?"

"What will you have, dear Frog?" said she. "My dresses, my pearls and jewels, or the golden crown which I wear?"

The Frog answered, "Dresses, or jewels, or golden crowns, are not for me, but if thou wilt love me, and let me by thy companion and playfellow, and sit at thy table, and eat from thy little golden plate, and drink out of thy

cup, and sleep in thy little bed, — if thou wilt promise me all these, then will I dive down and fetch up thy golden ball."

"Oh, I will promise you all," said she, "if you will only get me my ball." But she thought to herself, "What is the silly Frog chattering about? Let him remain in the water with his equals; he cannot mix in society." But the Frog, as soon as he had received her promise, drew his head under the water and dived down. Presently he swam up again with the ball in his mouth, and threw it on the grass. The King's daughter was full of joy when she again saw her beautiful plaything; and, taking it up, she ran off immediately. "Stop! stop!" cried the Frog; "take me with thee. I cannot run as thou canst." But all his croaking was useless; although it was loud enough, the King's daughter did not hear it, but, hastening home, soon forgot the poor Frog, who was obliged to leap back into the fountain.

The next day, when the King's daughter was sitting at table with her father and all his courtiers, and was eating from her own little golden plate, something was heard coming up the marble stairs, splish-splash, splish-splash; and when it arrived at the top, it knocked at the door, and a voice said, "Open the door, thou youngest daughter of the King!" So she rose and went to see who it was that called her; but when she opened the door and caught sight of the Frog, she shut it again with great vehemence, and sat down at the table, looking very pale. But the King per-

44

ceived that her heart was beating violently, and asked her whether it were a giant who had come to fetch her away who stood at the door. "Oh, no!" answered she; "it is no giant, but an ugly Frog."

"What does the Frog want with you?" said the King.

"Oh, dear father, when I was sitting yesterday playing by the fountain, my golden ball fell into the water, and this Frog fetched it up again because I cried so much: but first, I must tell you, he pressed me so much, that I promised him he should be my companion. I never thought that he could come out of the water, but somehow he has jumped out, and now he wants to come in here."

At that moment there was another knock, and a voice said, —

> "King's daughter, youngest,
>   Open the door.
> Hast thou forgotten
> Thy promises made
> At the fountain so clear
> 'Neath the lime-tree's shade?
> King's daughter, youngest,
>   Open the door."

Then the King said, "What you have promised, that you must perform; go and let him in." So the King's daughter went and opened the door, and the Frog hopped in after her right up to her chair: and as soon as she was seated, the Frog said, "Take me up;" but she hesitated so long that at last the King ordered her to obey. And as soon

as the Frog sat on the chair, he jumped on to the table, and said, "Now push thy plate near me, that we may eat together." And she did so, but as everyone saw, very unwillingly. The Frog seemed to relish his dinner much, but every bit that the King's daughter ate nearly choked her, till at last the Frog said. "I have satisfied my hunger and feel very tired; wilt thou carry me upstairs now into thy chamber, and make thy bed ready that we may sleep together?" At this speech the King's daughter began to cry, for she was afraid of the cold Frog, and dared not touch him; and besides, he actually wanted to sleep in her own beautiful, clean bed.

But her tears only made the King very angry, and he said, "He who helped you in the time of your trouble, must not now be despised!" So she took the Frog up with two fingers, and put him in a corner of her chamber. But as she lay in her bed, he crept up to it, and said, "I am so very tired that I shall sleep well; do take me up or I will tell thy father." This speech put the King's daughter in a terrible passion, and catching the Frog up, she threw him with all her strength against the wall, saying, "Now, will you be quiet, you ugly Frog?"

But as he fell he was changed from a frog into a handsome Prince with beautiful eyes, who, after a little while became, with her father's consent, her dear companion and betrothed. Then he told her how he had been transformed by an evil witch, and that no one but herself could have

48

had the power to take him out of the fountain; and that on the morrow they would go together into his own kingdom.

The next morning, as soon as the sun rose, a carriage drawn by eight white horses, with ostrich feathers on their heads, and golden bridles, drove up to the door of the palace, and behind the carriage stood the trusty Henry, the servant of the young Prince. When his master was changed into a frog, trusty Henry had grieved so much that he had bound three iron bands round his heart, for fear it should break with grief and sorrow. But now that the carriage was ready to carry the young Prince to his own country, the faithful Henry helped in the bride and bridegroom, and placed himself in the seat behind, full of joy at his master's release. They had not proceeded far when the Prince heard a crack as if something had broken behind the carriage; so he put his head out of the window and asked Henry what was broken, and Henry answered, "It was not the carriage, my master, but a band which I bound round my heart when it was in such grief because you changed into a frog."

Twice afterwards on the journey there was the same noise, and each time the Prince thought that it was some part of the carriage that had given way; but it was only the breaking of the bands which bound the heart of the trusty Henry, who was thence-forward free and happy.

GOODY TWO SHOES

IN the reign of good Queen Bess, there was an honest, industrious countryman named Meanwell, who, living under a hard landlord, was cruelly turned out of his little farm, which had enabled him to support a wife and two children, called Tommy and Margery. Care and misfortune soon shortened his days; and his wife, not long after, followed him to the grave. At her death the two poor children were left in a sad plight, and had to make all sorts of shifts to keep themselves from starving. They were also without proper clothes to keep them warm; and as for shoes, they had not even two pairs between them: Tommy, who had to go about more than his sister, had a pair to himself, but little Margery for a long time wore but one shoe.

But Heaven had heard their dying mother's prayers, and had watched over and protected them. Relief was at hand, and better things were in store for them. It happened that Mr. Goodall, the clergyman of the parish, heard of their sad wandering sort of life, and so he sent for the two children, and kindly offered to shelter them until they could get regular work to do. Soon after this, a gentleman came from London on a visit, and no sooner did he hear the story of the orphans, than he resolved to be their friend. The very first thing he did was to order a pair of shoes to be made for Margery. And he offered to take Tommy to London, promising to put him in a way to do well by going abroad.

As these two children loved each other very dearly, Margery was in great trouble when the time came for her brother to start, and wept bitterly. But Tommy, in order to comfort her, promised he would not fail to come back to see her, when he should return from foreign countries.

After he was gone, Margery began to recover her usual cheerfulness: but what helped greatly to put her into good spirits, was the pleasure she took in her new shoes. As soon as the old shoemaker brought them, she put them on, and ran at once to the clergyman's wife, crying out with glee, as she pointed to them, "Two shoes, ma'am! See, Two shoes!" These words she kept on repeating to everybody she met, and so came to be called GOODY TWO SHOES.

Now Margery was a thoughtful little girl, and was most anxious to learn to read and write. When Mr. Goodall saw this, he kindly taught her what she most wished to know, and in a short time she became a better scholar than any of the children who went to the village school. As soon as she found that this was the case, she thought she would try to teach such poor children as could not go to school. Now, as very few books were then printed, she thought she could get over the difficulty by cutting, out of wood, six sets of capital letters like these:—

A B C D E F G H I J K L M N O P Q R S T U V W X Y Z.
And ten sets of these common letters:—

a b c d e f g h i j k l m n o p q r s t u v w x y z.

When, after much pains and trouble, she had finished all these wooden letters, she managed to borrow an old spelling-book, and, with the help of this, she made her playmates set up the words she wished them to spell.

One day, as Margery was coming home from the next village, she met with some wicked, idle boys, who had tied a young raven to a staff, and were just going to throw stones at it. She offered at once to buy the raven for a penny, and this they agreed to. She then brought him home to the parsonage, and gave him the name of Ralph, and a fine bird he was. Madge soon taught him to speak several words, and also to pick up letters, and even to spell a word or two.

Some years before Margery began to teach the poor

cottagers' children, Sir Walter Welldon, a wealthy knight, had set up an elderly widow lady in a small school in the village. This gentlewoman was at length taken ill, and was no longer able to attend to her duties. When Sir Walter heard of this, he sent for Mr. Goodall, and asked him to look out for some one who would be able and willing to take Mrs. Gray's place as mistress of the school.

The worthy clergyman could think of no one so well qualified for the task as Margery Meanwell, who, though but young, was grave beyond her years, and was growing up to be a comely maiden; and when he told his mind to the knight, Margery was at once chosen. Sir Walter built a larger school-house for Margery's use; so that she could have all her old pupils about her that liked to come, as well as the regular scholars.

From this time, no one called her "Goody Two Shoes," but generally Mrs. Margery, and she was more and more liked and respected by her neighbours.

Soon after Margery had become mistress of the school, she saved a dove from some cruel boys, and she called him Tom, in remembrance of her brother now far away, and from whom she had heard no tidings.

About this time a lamb had lost its dam, and its owner was about to have it killed; when Margery heard of this, she bought the lamb and brought it home. Some neighbours, finding how fond of such pets Margery was, presented her with a nice playful little dog called Jumper, and

56

also with a skylark. Now, master Ralph was a shrewd bird, and a bit of a wag too, and when Will, the lamb, and Carol, the lark, made their appearance, the knowing fellow picked out the following verse, to the great amusement of every-body:—

> "Early to bed, and early to rise,
> Is the way to be healthy, wealthy and wise."

Mrs. Margery was ever on the look-out to be useful to her neighbours. Now a traveller from London had pre-sented her with a new kind of instrument, a rough-looking barometer, by the help of which she could often guess correctly how the weather would be, a day or two before-hand. This caused a great talk about the country, and so provoked were the people of the distant villages at the better luck of the Mouldwell folks, that they accused Mrs. Margery of being a witch, and sent old Nicky Noodle to go and tax her with it, and to scrape together whatever evidence he could against her. When this wiseacre saw her at her school-door, with her raven on one shoulder and the dove on the other, the lark on her hand, and the lamb and little dog by her side, the sight took his breath away for a time, and he scampered off, crying out, "A witch, a witch, a witch!"

She laughed at the simpleton's folly, and called him jocosely a "conjuror!" for his pains; but poor Mrs. Margery did not know how much folly and wickedness there was in the world, and she was greatly surprised to find that the

half-witted Nicky Noodle had got a warrant against her.

At the meeting of the justices, before whom she was summoned to appear, many of her neighbours were present, ready to speak up for her chracter if needful. But it turned out that the charge made against her was nothing more than Nicky's idle tale that she was a witch. Now-a-days it seems strange that such a thing could be; but in England, at that period, so fondly styled by some "the good old times," many silly and wicked things were constantly being done, especially by the rich and powerful against the poor — such things as would not now be borne.

It happened that, among the justices who met to hear this charge against Mrs. Margery, there was but one silly enough to think there was any ground for it; his name was Shallow, and it was he who had granted the warrant. But she soon silenced him when he kept repeating that she *must* be a witch to foretell the weather, besides harbouring many strange creatures about her, by explaining the use of her weather-glass.

Fortunately her patron, Sir Walter Welldon, was well acquainted with the use of the new instrument. When he had explained its nature to his foolish brother-justice, he turned the whole charge into ridicule, and gave Mrs. Margery such a high character, that the justices not only released her at once, but gave her their public thanks for the good services she had done in their neighbourhood.

One of these gentlemen, Sir Edward Lovell, who was

61

a widower, fell ill, and requested Mrs. Margery to take charge of his house, and look after his dear children. Having taken counsel with her kind old friend the clergyman, she consented to this, and quite won Sir Edward's respect and admiration by her skill and tenderness in nursing him, and by the great care she took of his children.

By the time that Sir Edward fully regained his health, he had become more and more attached to Mrs. Margery. It was not then to be wondered at, that when she talked of going back to her school, he should offer her his hand in marriage. This proposal took her quite by surprise, but she really loved Sir Edward; and her friends, Sir Walter and Mr. Goodall, advised her to accept him, telling her she would then be able to do many more good works than she had ever done before.

All things having been settled, and the day fixed, the great folks and others in the neighbourhood came in crowds to see the wedding, for glad they were that one who had, ever since she was a child, been so deserving, was to be thus rewarded. Just as the bride and bridegroom were about to enter the church, their friends assembled outside were busily engaged in watching the progress of a horseman, handsomely dressed and mounted, who was galloping up a distant slope leading to the church, as eagerly as if he wanted to get there before the marriage. This gentleman, so elegantly dressed, proved to be no other than Margaret's brother, our former acquaintance little Tommy,

just returned with great honour and profit from a distant foreign country. When they had recovered from this pleasant surprise, the loving couple returned to the altar, and were married, to the satisfaction of all present.

After her happy marriage, Lady Lovell continued to practise all kinds of good; and took great pains in increasing and improving the school of which she had been the mistress, and placed there a poor but worthy scholar and his wife to preside over it.

A CHILD'S GARDEN OF VERSES

ROBERT LOUIS STEVENSON
WITH ILLUSTRATIONS BY
JESSIE WILLCOX SMITH

THE GROLIER SOCIETY INC. • NEW YORK

© The Grolier Society 1967

E F G H I J K   8 9

CONTENTS

BED IN SUMMER

IN winter I get up at night
And dress by yellow candle-light.
In summer, quite the other way,
I have to go to bed by day.

I have to go to bed and see
The birds still hopping on the tree,
Or hear the grown-up people's feet
Still going past me in the street.

And does it not seem hard to you,
When all the sky is clear and blue,
And I should like so much to play,
To have to go to bed by day?

AT THE SEA-SIDE

WHEN I was down beside the sea
 A wooden spade they gave to me
To dig the sandy shore.

My holes were empty like a cup.
In every hole the sea came up,
 Till it could come no more.

A GOOD PLAY

WE built a ship upon the stairs
       All made of the back-bedroom chairs,
And filled it full of sofa pillows
To go a-sailing on the billows.

We took a saw and several nails,
And water in the nursery pails;
And Tom said, "Let us also take
An apple and a slice of cake;"—
Which was enough for Tom and me
To go a-sailing on, till tea.

We sailed along for days and days
And had the very best of plays;
But Tom fell out and hurt his knee,
So there was no one left but me.

UP into the cherry tree
   Who should climb but little me?
I held the trunk with both my hands
And looked abroad on foreign lands.

I saw the next door garden lie,
Adorned with flowers, before my eye,
And many pleasant places more
That I had never seen before.

I saw the dimpling river pass
And be the sky's blue looking-glass;
The dusty roads go up and down
With people tramping in to town.

If I could find a higher tree
Farther and farther I should see,
To where the grown-up river slips
Into the sea among the ships,

To where the roads on either hand
Lead onward into fairy land,
Where all the children dine at five,
And all the playthings come alive.

SYSTEM

EVERY night my prayers I say,
And get my dinner every day;
And every day that I've been good,
I get an orange after food.

The child that is not clean and neat,
With lots of toys and things to eat,
He is a naughty child, I'm sure—
Or else his dear papa is poor.

A GOOD BOY

I WOKE before the morning, I was happy all the day,
I never said an ugly word, but smiled and stuck to play.

And now at last the sun is going down behind the wood,
And I am very happy, for I know that I've been good.

My bed is waiting cool and fresh, with linen smooth and fair
And I must be off to sleepsin-by, and not forget my prayer.

I know that, till to-morrow I shall see the sun arise,
No ugly dream shall fright my mind, no ugly sight my eyes.

But slumber hold me tightly till I waken in the dawn,
And hear the thrushes singing in the lilacs round the lawn.

THE LAND OF COUNTERPANE

WHEN I was sick and lay a-bed,
    I had two pillows at my head,
And all my toys beside me lay
To keep me happy all the day.

And sometimes for an hour or so
I watched my leaden soldiers go,
With different uniforms and drills,
Among the bed-clothes, through the hills;

And sometimes sent my ships in fleets
All up and down among the sheets;
Or brought my trees and houses out,
And planted cities all about.

I was the giant great and still
That sits upon the pillow-hill,
And sees before him, dale and plain,
The pleasant land of counterpane.

MARCHING SONG

BRING the comb and play upon it!
　　Marching, here we come!
Willie cocks his highland bonnet,
　　Johnnie beats the drum.

Mary Jane commands the party,
　　Peter leads the rear;
Feet in time, alert and hearty,
　　Each a Grenadier!

All in the most martial manner
　　Marching double-quick;
While the napkin, like a banner,
　　Waves upon the stick!

Here's enough of fame and pillage,
　　Great commander Jane!
Now that we've been round the village,
　　Let's go home again.

HAPPY THOUGHT

THE world is so full of a number of things,
I'm sure we should all be as happy as kings.

MY SHADOW

I HAVE a little shadow that goes in and out with me,
And what can be the use of him is more than I can see.
He is very, very like me from the heels up to the head;
And I see him jump before me, when I jump into my bed.

The funniest thing about him is the way he likes to grow—
Not at all like proper children, which is always very slow;
For he sometimes shoots up taller like an india-rubber ball,
And he sometimes gets so little that there's none of him at all.

He hasn't got a notion of how children ought to play,
And can only make a fool of me in every sort of way.
He stays so close beside me, he's a coward you can see;
I'd think shame to stick to nursie as that shadow sticks to me!

One morning, very early, before the sun was up,
I rose and found the shining dew on every buttercup;
But my lazy little shadow, like an arrant sleepy-head,
Had stayed at home behind me and was fast asleep in bed.

THE WIND

I SAW you toss the kites on high
  And blow the birds about the sky;
And all around I heard you pass,
Like ladies' skirts across the grass—
  O wind, a-blowing all day long,
  O wind, that sings so loud a song!

I saw the different things you did,
But always you yourself you hid.
I felt you push, I heard you call,
I could not see yourself at all—
  O wind, a-blowing all day long,
  O wind, that sings so loud a song!

O you that are so strong and cold,
O blower, are you young or old?
Are you a beast of field and tree,
Or just a stronger child than me?
  O wind, a-blowing all day long,
  O wind, that sings so loud a song!

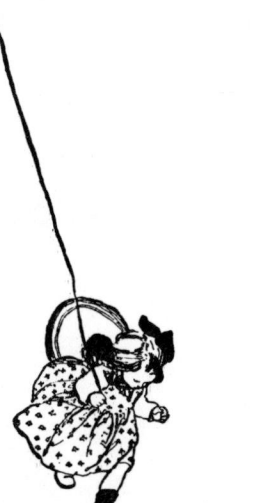

FOREIGN CHILDREN

LITTLE Indian, Sioux or Crow,
   Little frosty Eskimo,
Little Turk or Japanee,
Oh! don't you wish that you were me?

You have seen the scarlet trees
And the lions over seas;
You have eaten ostrich eggs,
And turned the turtles off their legs.

Such a life is very fine,
But it's not so nice as mine:
You must often, as you trod,
Have wearied *not* to be abroad.

You have curious things to eat,
I am fed on proper meat;
You must dwell beyond the foam,
But I am safe and live at home.
  Little Indian, Sioux or Crow,
  Little frosty Eskimo,
  Little Turk or Japanee,
Oh! don't you wish that you were me?

THE MOON

THE moon has a face like the clock in the hall
   She shines on thieves on the garden wall,
On streets and field and harbour quays,
And birdies asleep in the forks of the trees.

The squalling cat and the squeaking mouse,
The howling dog by the door of the house,
The bat that lies in bed at noon,
All love to be out by the light of the moon.

But all of the things that belong to the day
Cuddle to sleep to be out of her way;
And flowers and children close their eyes
Till up in the morning the sun shall arise.

TO AUNTIE

CHIEF *of our aunts—not only I,*
    But all your dozen of nurselings cry—
What did the other children do?
And what were childhood, wanting you?

THE UNSEEN PLAYMATE

WHEN children are playing alone on the green,
In comes the playmate that never was seen.
When children are happy and lonely and good,
The Friend of the Children comes out of the wood.

Nobody heard him and nobody saw,
His is a picture you never could draw,
But he's sure to be present, abroad or at home,
When children are happy and playing alone.

He lies in the laurels, he runs on the grass,
He sings when you tinkle the musical glass;
Whene'er you are happy and cannot tell why,
The Friend of the Children is sure to be by!

He loves to be little, he hates to be big,
'Tis he that inhabits the caves that you dig;
'Tis he when you play with your soldiers of tin
That sides with the Frenchmen and never can win.

'Tis he, when at night you go off to your bed,
Bids you go to your sleep and not trouble your head;
For wherever they're lying, in cupboard or shelf,
'Tis he will take care of your playthings himself!

LOOKING-GLASS RIVER

SMOOTH it glides upon its travel,
   Here a wimple, there a gleam—
    O the clean gravel!
    O the smooth stream!

Sailing blossoms, silver fishes,
   Paven pools as clear as air—
    How a child wishes
    To live down there!

We can see our coloured faces
   Floating on the shaken pool
    Down in cool places,
    Dim and very cool;

Till a wind or water wrinkle,
   Dipping marten, plumping trout,
    Spreads in a twinkle
    And blots all out.

See the rings pursue each other;
All below grows black as night,
Just as if mother
Had blown out the light!

Patience, children, just a minute—
See the spreading circles die;
The stream and all in it
Will clear by-and-by.

AUTUMN FIRES

IN the other gardens
    And all up the vale,
From the autumn bonfires
    See the smoke trail!

Pleasant summer over
    And all the summer flowers,
The red fire blazes,
    The grey smoke towers.

Sing a song of seasons!
    Something bright in all!
Flowers in the summer,
    Fires in the fall!

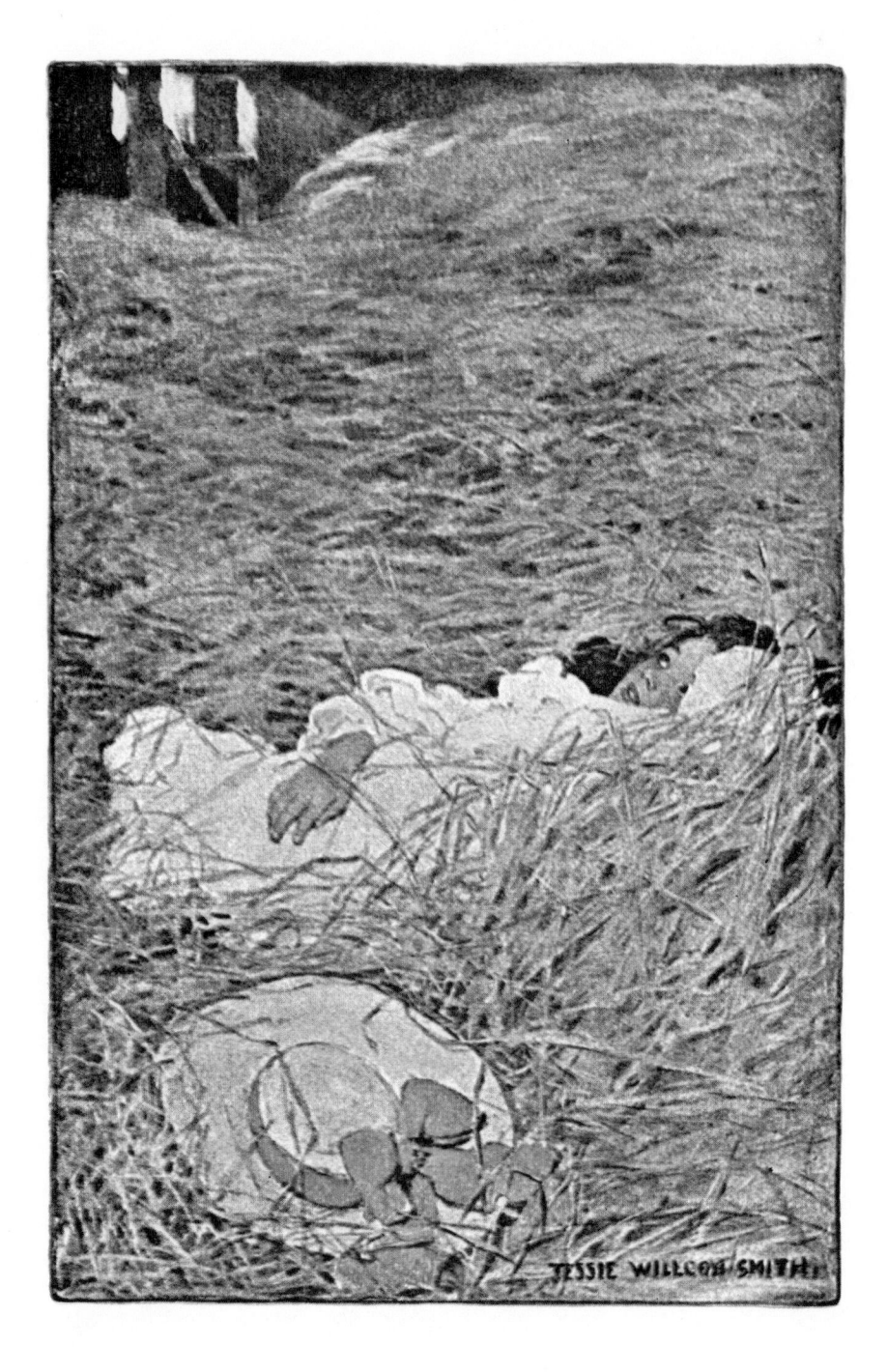

THE HAYLOFT

THROUGH all the pleasant meadow-side
  The grass grew shoulder-high,
Till the shining scythes went far and wide
  And cut it down to dry.

Those green and sweetly smelling crops
  They led in waggons home;
And they piled them here in mountain tops
  For mountaineers to roam.

Here is Mount Clear, Mount Rusty-Nail,
  Mount Eagle and Mount High;—
The mice that in these mountains dwell,
  No happier are than I!

Oh, what a joy to clamber there,
    Oh, what a place for play,
With the sweet, the dim, the dusty air,
    The happy hills of hay!

WINTER-TIME

LATE lies the wintry sun a-bed,
  A frosty, fiery sleepy-head;
Blinks but an hour or two; and then,
A blood-red orange, sets again.

Before the stars have left the skies,
At morning in the dark I rise;
And shivering in my nakedness,
By the cold candle, bathe and dress.

Close by the jolly fire I sit
To warm my frozen bones a bit;
Or with a reindeer-sled, explore
The colder countries round the door.

When to go out, my nurse doth wrap
Me in my comforter and cap;
The cold wind burns my face, and blows
Its frosty pepper up my nose.

Black are my steps on silver sod;
Thick blows my frosty breath abroad;
And tree and house, and hill and lake,
Are frosted like a wedding-cake.

NORTH-WEST PASSAGE

1. Good-night

WHEN the bright lamp is carried in,
The sunless hours again begin;
O'er all without, in field and lane,
The haunted night returns again.

Now we behold the embers flee
About the firelit hearth; and see
Our faces painted as we pass,
Like pictures, on the window-glass.

Must we to bed indeed? Well then,
Let us arise and go like men,
And face with an undaunted tread
The long black passage up to bed.

Farewell, O brother, sister, sire!
O pleasant party round the fire!
The songs you sing, the tales you tell,
Till far to-morrow, fare ye well!

2. Shadow March

All round the house is the jet-black night;
   It stares through the window-pane;
It crawls in the corners, hiding from the light,
   And it moves with the moving flame.

Now my little heart goes a-beating like a drum,
   With the breath of the Bogie in my hair;
And all round the candle the crooked shadows come,
   And go marching along up the stair.

The shadow of the balusters, the shadow of the lamp,
   The shadow of the child that goes to bed—
All the wicked shadows coming, tramp, tramp, tramp,
   With the black night overhead.

3. *In Port*

Last, to the chamber where I lie
My fearful footsteps patter nigh,
And come from out the cold and gloom
Into my warm and cheerful room.

There, safe arrived, we turn about
To keep the coming shadows out,
And close the happy door at last
On all the perils that we past.

Then, when mamma goes by to bed,
She shall come in with tip-toe tread,
And see me lying warm and fast
And in the Land of Nod at last.

THE LITTLE LAND

WHEN at home alone I sit,
And am very tired of it,
I have just to shut my eyes
To go sailing through the skies—
To go sailing far away
To the pleasant Land of Play;
To the fairy land afar
Where the Little People are;
Where the clover-tops are trees,
And the rain-pools are the seas,
And the leaves, like little ships,
Sail about on tiny trips;
And above the daisy tree
Through the grasses,
High o'erhead the Bumble Bee
Hums and passes.

In that forest to and fro
I can wander, I can go;
See the spider and the fly,
And the ants go marching by;

41

Carrying parcels with their feet
Down the green and grassy street.
I can in the sorrel sit
Where the ladybird alit.
I can climb the jointed grass
   And on high
See the greater swallows pass
   In the sky,
And the round sun rolling by
Heeding no such things as I.

Through that forest I can pass
Till, as in a looking-glass,
Humming fly and daisy tree
And my tiny self I see,
Painted very clear and neat
On the rain-pool at my feet.
Should a leaflet come to land
Drifting near to where I stand,
Straight I'll board that tiny boat
Round the rain-pool sea to float.

Little thoughtful creatures sit
On the grassy coasts of it;
Little things with lovely eyes
See me sailing with surprise.
Some are clad in armour green—
(These have sure to battle been!)—
Some are pied with ev'ry hue,
Black and crimson, gold and blue;

Some have wings and swift are gone;—
But they all look kindly on.

When my eyes I once again
Open, and see all things plain:
High bare walls, great bare floor;
Great big knobs on drawer and door;
Great big people perched on chairs,
Stitching tucks and mending tears,
Each a hill that I could climb,
And talking nonsense all the time—
O dear me,
That I could be
A sailor on the rain-pool sea,
A climber in the clover tree,
And just come back, a sleepy-head,
Late at night to go to bed.

MY TREASURES

THESE nuts, that I keep in the back of the nest
Where all my lead soldiers are lying at rest,
Were gathered in autumn by nursie and me
In a wood with a well by the side of the sea.

This whistle we made (and how clearly it sounds!)
By the side of a field at the end of the grounds.
Of a branch of a plane, with a knife of my own,
It was nursie who made it, and nursie alone!

The stone, with the white and the yellow and grey,
We discovered I cannot tell *how* far away;
And I carried it back although weary and cold,
For though father denies it, I'm sure it is gold.

But of all my treasures the last is the king,
For there's very few children possess such a thing;
And that is a chisel, both handle and blade,
Which a man who was really a carpenter made.

SUMMER fading, winter comes—
Frosty mornings, tingling thumbs,
Window robins, winter rooks,
And the picture story-books.

Water now is turned to stone
Nurse and I can walk upon;
Still we find the flowing brooks
In the picture story-books.

All the pretty things put by,
Wait upon the children's eye,
Sheep and shepherds, trees and crooks,
In the picture story-books.

We may see how all things are,
Seas and cities, near and far,
And the flying fairies' looks,
In the picture story-books.

How am I to sing your praise,
Happy chimney-corner days,
Sitting safe in nursery nooks,
Reading picture story-books?

BLOCK CITY

WHAT are you able to build with your blocks?
Castles and palaces, temples and docks.
Rain may keep raining, and others go roam,
But I can be happy and building at home.

Let the sofa be mountains, the carpet be sea,
There I'll establish a city for me:
A kirk and a mill and a palace beside,
And a harbour as well where my vessels may ride.

Great is the palace with pillar and wall,
A sort of a tower on the top of it all,
And steps coming down in an orderly way
To where my toy vessels lie safe in the bay.

This one is sailing and that one is moored:
Hark to the song of the sailors on board!
And see, on the steps of my palace, the kings
Coming and going with presents and things!

Now I have done with it, down let it go!
All in a moment the town is laid low.
Block upon block lying scattered and free,
What is there left of my town by the sea?

Yet as I saw it, I see it again,
The kirk and the palace, the ships and the men,
And as long as I live and where'er I may be,
I'll always remember my town by the sea.

THE LAND OF STORY–BOOKS

AT evening when the lamp is lit,
    Around the fire my parents sit;
They sit at home and talk and sing,
    And do not play at anything.

Now, with my little gun, I crawl
All in the dark along the wall,
And follow round the forest track
Away behind the sofa back.

There, in the night, where none can spy,
All in my hunter's camp I lie,
And play at books that I have read
Till it is time to go to bed.

These are the hills, these are the woods,
These are my starry solitudes;
And there the river by whose brink
The roaring lions come to drink.

I see the others far away
As if in firelit camp they lay,
And I, like to an Indian scout,
Around their party prowled about.

So, when my nurse comes in for me,
Home I return across the sea,
And go to bed with backward looks
At my dear land of Story-books.

THE FLOWERS

ALL the names I know from nurse:
   Gardener's garters, Shepherd's purse,
Bachelor's buttons, Lady's smock,
And the Lady Hollyhock.

Fairy places, fairy things,
Fairy woods where the wild bee wings,
Tiny trees for tiny dames—
These must all be fairy names!

Tiny woods below whose boughs
Shady fairies weave a house;
Tiny tree-tops, rose or thyme,
Where the braver fairies climb!

Fair are grown-up people's trees,
But the fairest woods are these;
Where, if I were not so tall,
I should live for good and all.

NIGHT AND DAY

WHEN the golden day is done,
   Through the closing portal,
Child and garden, flower and sun,
   Vanish all things mortal.

As the blinding shadows fall
   As the rays diminish,
Under evening's cloak, they all
   Roll away and vanish.

Garden darkened, daisy shut,
   Child in bed, they slumber—
Glow-worm in the highway rut,
   Mice among the lumber.

In the darkness houses shine,
   Parents move with candles;
Till on all, the night divine
   Turns the bedroom handles.

Till at last the day begins
  In the east a-breaking,
In the hedges and the whins
  Sleeping birds a-waking.

In the darkness shapes of things,
  Houses, trees and hedges,
Clearer grow; and sparrow's wings
  Beat on window ledges.

These shall wake the yawning maid;
  She the door shall open—
Finding dew on garden glade
  And the morning broken.

There my garden grows again
  Green and rosy painted,
As at eve behind the pane
  From my eyes it fainted.

Just as it was shut away,
  Toy-like, in the even,
Here I see it glow with day
  Under glowing heaven.

Every path and every plot,
  Every bush of roses,
Every blue forget-me-not
  Where the dew reposes.

"Up!" they cry, "the day is come
    On the smiling valleys:
We have beat the morning drum;
    Playmate, join your allies!"

THE SWING

HOW do you like to go up in a swing,
   Up in the air so blue?
Oh, I do think it the pleasantest thing
   Ever a child can do!

Up in the air and over the wall,
   Till I can see so wide,
Rivers and trees and cattle and all
   Over the countryside—

Till I look down on the garden green,
   Down on the roof so brown—
Up in the air I go flying again,
   Up in the air and down!

TIME TO RISE

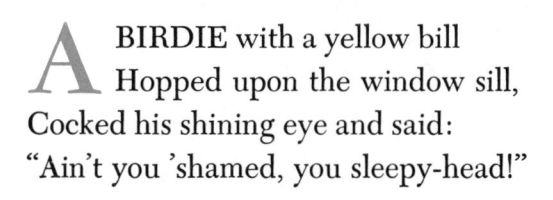

A BIRDIE with a yellow bill
Hopped upon the window sill,
Cocked his shining eye and said:
"Ain't you 'shamed, you sleepy-head!"

MY KINGDOM

DOWN by a shining water well
    I found a very little dell,
      No higher than my head.
The heather and the gorse about
In summer bloom were coming out,
      Some yellow and some red.

I called the little pool a sea;
The little hills were big to me;
      For I am very small.

I made a boat, I made a town,
I searched the caverns up and down,
  And named them one and all.

And all about was mine, I said,
The little sparrows overhead,
  The little minnows too.
This was the world and I was king;
For me the bees came by to sing,
  For me the swallows flew.

I played there were no deeper seas,
Nor any wider plains than these,
  Nor other kings than me.
At last I heard my mother call
Out from the house at evenfall,
  To call me home to tea.

And I must rise and leave my dell,
And leave my dimpled water well,
  And leave my heather blooms.
Alas! and as my home I neared,
How very big my nurse appeared.
  How great and cool the rooms!